The Tap Dance Mystery

TO: MRS. SALTZMAN

The Tap Dance Mystery

by **Susan Pearson**

illustrated by **Gioia Fiammenghi**

SIMON AND SCHUSTER BOOKS FOR YOUNG READERS
PUBLISHED BY SIMON & SCHUSTER INC.
New York • London • Toronto • Sydney • Tokyo • Singapore

SIMON AND SCHUSTER BOOKS FOR YOUNG READERS
Simon & Schuster Building, Rockefeller Center, 1230 Avenue of the Americas, New York,
New York 10020. Text copyright © 1990 by Susan Pearson. Illustrations copyright © 1990
by Gioia Fiammenghi. All rights reserved including the right of reproduction in whole or
in part in any form. SIMON AND SCHUSTER BOOKS FOR YOUNG READERS is a trademark of
Simon & Schuster Inc.
Designed by Lucille Chomowicz
Manufactured in the United States of America
10 9 8 7 6 5 4 3 2 1   pbk. 10 9 8 7 6 5 4 3 2
Library of Congress Cataloging-in-Publication Data: Pearson, Susan. The tap dance
mystery. Summary: Amidst the school's preparation for Parent's Night, Eagle-Eye Ernie
solves the mystery of a pair of missing tap shoes. [1. Mystery and detective stories.]
I. Fiammenghi, Gioia, ill. II. Title. III. Title: Tap dance mystery.
PZ7.P323316Eb 1990 [Fic]—dc20 89-48017
ISBN 0-671-70566-0 ISBN 0-671-70570-9 (pbk.)

To Richard Trombley,
for the gift of time—SP

To Laura —GF

CONTENTS

CHAPTER 1

Dance or Quit

"We dance or I quit!" said Marcie.

She was standing with her hands on her hips. The rest of the group—Ernie, William, and Jason—were sitting on the gym floor.

"You can't quit," said Ernie. "Ms. Finney said everyone has to be in the act."

"Then dance," said Marcie. She jerked her head. Her yellow hair bounced.

"But Marcie," said William. "We don't know how."

"I will teach you," said Marcie.

Ernie groaned. She knew what *that* would be like.

"We don't have shoes," said Ernie. "You are the only one with tap shoes."

"That's okay," said Marcie. "You can do the steps. I will make all the taps. That way it will sound as if we are all together. Even when you make mistakes."

"What about costumes?" said Ernie. "You are the only one with a costume."

"You can make your own," said Marcie. "I will bring mine to school. You can copy it."

Ernie didn't like the sound of that. It sounded like a lot of work—a lot of work for her and William and Jason, that is.

It wasn't that Ernie minded working hard. She didn't. She just thought everyone should work hard. At least, everyone in this group.

"We would have to learn the steps," she

said. "And we would have to make our costumes. What would you have to do, Marcie?"

Marcie smiled her sweet, sticky smile. It was not a friendly smile. It smelled like Juicy Fruit gum. Ernie hated that smell. She had to smell it every single day. Marcie sat right in front of her in Ms. Finney's room.

"I have the hardest job of all," said Marcie. "I have to teach you how to tap dance."

Ernie groaned again. Marcie teaching meant Marcie bossing around.

Ernie looked at William. His finger was drawing invisible pictures on the floor. William was always drawing.

She looked at Jason. He was staring at the floor, too. He wasn't drawing pictures. He was just staring.

"Let's vote," said Marcie.

Ernie sighed. "All right," she said. "How many want to dance?"

Marcie and William and Jason raised their hands.

Ernie could not believe it.

"*Jason!*" she said.

Jason wiped his nose on his sleeve. He did not look up.

"I want to learn how to dance," he whispered. Jason always whispered. Ernie wondered what made him so shy.

"*William!*" said Ernie.

William rubbed the lucky rabbit he wore around his neck. Then he looked at Ernie.

"I don't want to fight," he said. He looked sorry.

"I win!" said Marcie.

She bounced her yellow hair again. Then she sat back down on the floor. She pulled a piece of paper and a pencil out of her backpack.

"Now here is what we will do," she said.

She began to write on the paper. Words like *slap* and *shuffle* and *ball change*. They didn't make any sense to Ernie.

They didn't make any sense to William either, Ernie guessed. He went back to drawing pictures on the floor.

Only Jason paid attention. He wasn't staring at the floor anymore. He was looking at Marcie's paper. His face looked happy. His toes were wiggling inside his shoes.

Ernie looked around the gym. She wished she was in Michael's group. Michael had his headphones on. She heard him say, "Mission Control says . . ." She couldn't hear the rest, but it must have been funny. The other kids in his group were all laughing.

Ernie looked over at R.T. R.T.'s real name was Rachel, but everyone called her R.T., even Ms. Finney. Her group was sitting close together. They were all leaning into the middle. They were whispering. R.T. was chewing on her braid. She did that when she was thinking. Ernie wished she was in R.T.'s group.

She wished she was anywhere but here.

CHAPTER 2

Bananas and Tap Shoes

Ernie trudged down the street. She was on her way to the Martian clubhouse. She was carrying a bag. Inside the bag were four bananas. Four bananas for four Martians.

The clubhouse was in Michael's backyard. The Martians often met there after school.

A sign on the door said:

MARTIAN CLUB
PRIVATE!
MARTIANS ONLY!
THIS MEANS
PRINCE MICHAEL
QUEEN ERNIE
KING WILLIAM
QUEEN R.T.
EVERYONE ELSE KEEP OUT!

Another sign said:

STAR FINDER
Travel Through Space
With Commander Michael

When it wasn't the clubhouse, the play-house was Michael's spaceship.

Ernie pushed open the door. Everyone was there already. And everyone was busy.

R.T. had brought Ralph. Ralph was her rabbit. She had also brought a big cowboy hat. She was trying to push Ralph into the hat. Ralph did not want to go.

R.T. pulled some lettuce out of her pocket. She put it inside the hat.

Ralph liked lettuce a lot. He jumped right into the hat. He ate the lettuce. Then he jumped right back out.

"Ralph!" R.T. scolded. "That is no way for a magic bunny to act! Get back in there!"

"Since when is Ralph a magic bunny?" Ernie asked.

"Since today," said R.T. "My group is doing magic tricks. We are the Magic Marvels."

"Oh," said Ernie. She wished again that she was in R.T.'s group.

"My group is Jupiter Jive," said Michael.

He opened a large cookie tin. He wrapped a long strip of cloth around it. Then he put the lid back on and tied a knot in the cloth. Michael wrapped the cloth around his waist. He tied another knot. The cookie tin was strapped to his back.

"Why do you want to wear a cookie tin?" asked Ernie.

"It's not a cookie tin," said Michael. "It's my drum."

"Funny place to wear a drum," said Ernie.

"No it's not," said Michael. "I will tie a wooden spoon to my arm. Then I can beat it behind me."

"Why not beat it in front of you with your hands?" said Ernie. "It would be a lot easier."

Michael looked at Ernie as if she were dumb.

"Because," he said, "I have to use my hands for other things. My group is a band from Jupiter. Jupiterians play lots of things at the same time."

Michael opened a plastic bottle. He dropped a bunch of things inside. Screws mostly. And some little round metal things with holes in the middle.

"What are those?" asked Ernie.

"Washers," said Michael. "My dad has hundreds of them in his tool box."

He screwed the cap back on the bottle. Then he shook it. The screws and washers rattled around inside.

"That sounds neat," said R.T.

"I know," said Michael. "I'm going to tie pan covers to my knees for cymbals."

"This is going to be the best Parents' Night ever!" said R.T. "Carmen's group is doing Stump the Parents. They are going to fool the parents with science tricks."

Ernie sighed. Things were looking worse and worse.

Maybe she could get sick. Anything would be better than being in this Parents' Night Show! There would be the Magic Marvels. Then there would be Jupiter Jive. Then there would be Stump the Parents. And then there would be Ernie and William and Jason and Marcie dancing.

Marcie would be wearing real tap shoes. Ernie would be wearing regular shoes. Marcie would be wearing a real costume.

11

Ernie would be wearing whatever she could find in her dress-up box. Ernie didn't like the look of it one bit.

Ernie looked over at William. He was sitting on the floor. An orange crate was his table. He was drawing away like mad. Pieces of paper were scattered all around him.

Ernie picked one up. It was a picture of a stage. The back curtain was covered with stars. There was a table at the front. It was covered with stars, too. R.T. was standing behind the table. She was pulling Ralph out of the cowboy hat.

"What are you doing?" Ernie asked.

"I am drawing the stage," said William. "I am going to change to Ellen's group. That is what they are doing—making the stage, announcing the acts, stuff like that. I am going to ask Ms. Finney tomorrow."

"You can't!" said Ernie. "Then it will be just me with Jason and Marcie. It will be worse than ever!"

"Yes I can," said William.

"What if I think of something?" said Ernie. "If I think of something, will you stay in our group?"

"You better think of something good," said William. He went back to drawing.

Ernie opened her bag. She pulled out a banana.

"Did you bring some for us?" asked Michael.

"Yes," said Ernie. "But you don't need them. Bananas are brain food. I need them all."

"That's not fair," said Michael. "I want a banana."

"You're not fair yourself, Michael," said R.T. "You ate all the cookies before Ernie even got here."

"Yeah," said William. "Leave Ernie alone. She has to think."

Michael put his Mission Control headphones on. He went back to work.

Ernie ate one banana. Then she ate another. Then she was full.

"Here," she said to Michael. She handed him the bag. "I can't eat any more bananas."

Ernie walked back and forth in the clubhouse. Back and forth. Back and forth.

"C'mon, brain food," she whispered. "Do your job."

She walked around R.T. She walked around William. She walked around Michael. She looked at R.T.'s hat. She looked at William's pictures. She looked at Michael's drum. She looked at Michael's noisy plastic bottle.

Suddenly, Ernie stopped short. She jumped into the air.

"*Bong!*" she shouted. That brain food worked every time.

"What is it?" shouted R.T.

"What are you going to do?" shouted Michael.

"It better be good," said William.

"It is!" shouted Ernie. "I need some of those washers, Michael," she said. "And some thumb tacks. And maybe a hammer."

"No problem," said Michael. "My dad has all that stuff. I'll go get it."

When Michael came back, Ernie got to work. She took off her shoes. She tacked three washers to the bottom of each toe. She tacked three more to the bottom of each heel. Then she pounded them in with the hammer.

Ernie put her shoes back on. She tied the laces. Then she brushed her toe on the floor.

Tap-tap.

She brushed her heel on the floor.

Tap-tap.

Ernie hopped on one foot. Then she hopped on the other. Then she skipped all around the clubhouse. *Tap-tap-tap-tap-tap-tap-tap-tap-tap-tap*. It worked! She sounded like a real tap dancer!

"Hooray for Ernie!" shouted R.T.

"I want some, too!" shouted Michael.

"Me first!" shouted William.

"Then you will stay in our group?" Ernie asked.

William rubbed his lucky rubber rabbit. "Sure," he said. "I guess so."

"You will be a wonderful tap dancer, William," said R.T. She was the one who had given William the lucky rabbit.

"Maybe," said William. "Just make sure you keep eating those bananas, Ernie."

CHAPTER 3

Ms. Finney's Woodpeckers

"I'm a clipper. I'm a clopper. I'm a clapper," Ernie sang on her way to school.

"I'm a hipper. I'm a hopper. I'm a happer. I'm a bipper. I'm a bopper. I'm a bapper. I'm a tipper. I'm a topper. I'M A TAPPER!"

Tap-tap went her shoes with every beat. *Tap-tap*, *tap-tap*, *tap-tap*.

Ernie hopped. She bopped. She clapped. She tapped.

She made a fancy turn at the corner. Just wait till Marcie saw that! Ernie was a tap dancer, too!

Ernie tapped into the schoolyard. She tapped straight to the jungle gym. She knew Marcie would be there.

Sure enough. There was Marcie sitting in the crow's nest, just like always. Marcie liked to be above everyone else.

There was Michael hanging by his knees, just like always, too. That was how Michael practiced being weightless.

"Hey, Marcie!" Ernie called. "Look at my tap shoes." Ernie did an extra fancy step to show off her shoes.

Marcie's mouth dropped open. "Those aren't tap shoes!" she yelled. "You can't wear those!"

"Sure she can," said Michael. "So can I!"

He dropped off the jungle gym. *Tap-tap, tap-tap, tap-tap*. He tapped over to Ernie. Michael had tacked washers onto his shoes, too!

Tap-tap, tap-tap, tap-tap, tap-tap. Who was tapping now?

Ernie and Michael turned around. There were R.T. and William. R.T.'s braids were swinging. William's grin filled his face.

"You can't do this!" yelled Marcie.

"Oh yes, we can!" said Ernie.

"What about me?" whispered Jason.

Ernie turned around. Jason wasn't on the jungle gym. He wasn't on the swings. Where was that whisper coming from?

Then Ernie spotted him. There were six old rubber tires next to the slide. Jason was curled into one of those. He had to bend up like a pretzel to fit.

Ernie opened her backpack. She pulled out a plastic bag. There were washers and tacks inside.

"I brought some taps for you, too," said Ernie.

Jason crawled out of the tire. He unbent himself. He wiped his nose on his sleeve.

"Oh boy!" he whispered.

Marcie climbed down from the crow's nest. She was wearing her backpack and carrying a cloth bag besides. It had a drawstring top. Ernie wondered what was in it.

"I'm telling Ms. Finney," said Marcie. "You are wrecking your shoes."

William looked at Ernie. He rubbed his lucky rabbit. He looked worried.

"We are not wrecking our shoes," said Ernie. "Tacks don't make big enough holes to wreck shoes."

"They do too," said Marcie. She held her bag close to her. "I'm telling."

"Go ahead," said William. "Ernie is right. Tacks make inky-dinky holes."

"Teeny-weeny Martian holes," said Michael.

"Itsy-bitsy mouse holes," said R.T.

Jason didn't say anything. He was pounding tacks into his shoes with a rock.

Just then the bell rang. Everyone ran inside. Ernie and William and Jason and R.T. and Michael tapped all the way.

"My goodness," said Ms. Finney when they came into the room. "What is all that tapping? Do we have woodpeckers in Room 123?"

"We are tap dancers," said Jason right out loud.

He wiped his nose on his sleeve. Then he tapped to his desk. His arms were waving. His shoulders were bouncing. His feet were flying.

Ernie was amazed. Jason was all loose. He looked rubbery. He looked like he had no bones. He looked *great*!

Ms. Finney must have thought so, too. "How long have you taken lessons?" she asked Jason.

"I don't take lessons," Jason whispered. He looked at the floor. "Only Marcie takes lessons."

Ms. Finney looked surprised.

"Only Marcie has real tap shoes, too," said William. "Ernie figured out how to make these. They aren't real. But they tap good."

"Our group is tap dancing for Parents' Night," Ernie explained.

"You can't wear those," said Marcie. "Can they, Ms. Finney? They will wreck their shoes. Tell them, Ms. Finney."

Ms. Finney asked Ernie to show her a shoe. She looked at it closely. Then she smiled.

"This is very clever, Ernie," she said. "And I don't think it will hurt your shoes. But it will hurt the floor. Tap shoes are for the gym only."

"But we didn't bring any other shoes," said Ernie.

Marcie smiled her sweet, sticky smile. "You will have to take the taps off these shoes," she said.

"I don't think that will be necessary," said Ms. Finney. "You can walk around in your socks for one day. Tomorrow you should wear other shoes. Just bring your tap shoes for practice."

Marcie glared at Ernie. Then she sat down at her desk. She opened her desk top. She tried to squeeze her bag inside her desk. It didn't fit.

Marcie slammed her desk shut. She put the bag under her chair. Then she sat very still and stared at the blackboard.

Ernie went to her desk. She took off her shoes. She put them into her backpack. She wiggled her toes in her socks. This was going to be a great day!

CHAPTER 4

Shuffle Off to Buffalo

Ernie liked sliding around in socks all day. She slid to the pencil sharpener. She slid to the art closet. She slid to the blackboard.

Finally Ms. Finney said, "That's enough sliding, Ernie."

Ernie was happy to stop by then. It was time to go practice in the gym anyway.

"You have all come up with wonderful acts," said Ms. Finney. "Now it is time for the real work. Practice!"

Ms. Finney pointed at the calendar.

"Parents' Night is a week from Friday," she said. "We will practice every day until then. Our room has the gym every day at one o'clock. We will practice there. Then we will have recess. Now line up and we'll get started."

Marcie reached under her desk. She picked up her bag. Then she got in line.

Ernie got in line right behind her. "What's in the bag, Marcie?" she asked.

Marcie smiled her sweet, sticky smile. The smell of Juicy Fruit gum blew into Ernie's face.

"You'll find out," said Marcie.

There were four groups in the gym. Each one got a corner.

The fifth group went to the workshop instead. They were building a stage. Mr. Winkler was helping them.

Ernie and William and Jason put their shoes back on.

"We're ready," Jason whispered. "Show us the dance."

"In a minute," said Marcie. She smiled her sweet, sticky smile. Then she opened her bag. She put her hand inside it. She bounced her yellow hair. Finally, she pulled two tap shoes out of the bag.

"Ooooooh," breathed Jason.

"Wow!" said William.

The shoes sparkled. You could see your face in them. They looked brand-new. They had black ribbons to tie them. Their taps were smooth and shiny.

"These are what *real* tap shoes look like," said Marcie.

Jason reached out his hand.

"Keep your hands off my shoes!" shouted Marcie.

"I just want to touch them," Jason whispered.

"Forget it," said Marcie.

Marcie put her shoes on. She stood up.

"And this is how you're *supposed* to tap dance," she said.

She danced to the middle of the gym. Her taps sounded clear and sharp. Next to them, Ernic's and William's and Jason's taps sounded scuffy.

Marcie's taps had something else, too. It was as if Ernie's and William's and Jason's taps were just words. Marcie's taps made sentences.

Soon the whole class was standing around Marcie. Their eyes were glued to Marcie's feet.

"Can I try them?" asked Sammy. His glasses were slipping down his nose. He didn't seem to know it.

"Oh, me first, *please*," said Geraldine. She hopped from one foot to the other.

"Ouch!" said Carmen. "You are squeezing my hand too tight, Geraldine. And you are standing on my foot."

"Me second!" said Tommy. His face was

very pink. His eyes looked like they might pop right out.

"No one can wear them but me," said Marcie. "You might wreck them."

Marcie put her hands on her hips. She danced around in a circle. Her feet tapped very fast.

What a show-off! thought Ernie.

"That's a fine dance, Marcie," said Ms. Finney. "I am sure that Ernie and Jason and William would like to learn it. Everyone get back to work now."

The kids went back to their groups. Marcie tapped all the way to Ernie's corner.

"First I'll teach you the slap," she said.

Tap-tap. She slapped the ball of her right foot on the floor. Then she slapped her left foot. Back and forth, right and left. *Tap-tap, tap-tap, tap-tap, tap-tap.*

The slap was easy! Ernie had been doing it all along. She just hadn't known what it was called.

"Next, the shuffle," said Marcie.

She swung her right foot forward. The tap brushed along the floor. Then she swung it back. The tap brushed again.

Forward-back, forward-back. *Brush-brush. Brush-brush*.

There was nothing to it. Tap dancing was easy as pie!

"And now," said Marcie, "we'll shuffle off to Buffalo."

Marcie shuffled. She hopped. She crossed one leg over the other. She shuffled and hopped and leg-crossed again. Off she went sideways across the floor. It sounded great, and it looked so easy.

Then Ernie tried it. She shuffled. Then she hopped. Oops—wrong foot. She shuffled again. She hopped. Now where did her leg go? Ernie was getting all tangled up.

William tried it next. He got all tangled up, too.

Then Jason tried it. Shuffle-hop-cross, shuffle-hop-cross, shuffle-hop-cross, shuffle-hop-cross. His taps made sentences now,

too. Off he went across the floor after Marcie. Their taps were exactly together. They looked like a matched set.

Ms. Finney blew her whistle. Marcie and Jason shuffle-hop-crossed back to Ernie and William.

"Don't watch your feet," said Marcie. She smiled her mean, sticky smile. "You two will have to practice at home. 'Shuffle off to Buffalo' is an important part of our dance."

Marcie changed her shoes fast. Then she ran down the hall after the other kids.

Ernie walked slowly and carefully so her taps wouldn't wreck the floor. Shuffle-hop-cross, shuffle-hop-cross. She tried to dance "Shuffle off to Buffalo" in her head.

On the playground, everyone was crowded around Marcie again.

"Please let me try them!" begged Geraldine.

"Just once," pleaded Sammy. His glasses were slipping again. He pushed them back up his nose.

"Come on, Marcie," said Tommy. He jumped up and down.

"Just let me touch them," whispered Jason.

Marcie held her shoe bag tighter.

"They're my shoes," she said. "You'll just wreck them."

Ernie felt disgusted. She went around the corner to practice "Shuffle off to Buffalo" in peace. She could still see Marcie, though.

"We won't wreck them," said Geraldine. "Will we, Carmen?"

"We'll be careful," said Sammy. "Honest we will."

"Yeah," said Tommy. He stopped jumping. His face was red.

Jason didn't say anything. He reached out his hand. He laid it gently on the shoe bag.

"Get your dirty hands off!" shouted Marcie. She ran back inside the school.

Shuffle-hop-cross. Shuffle-hop-cross. Ernie stared at her feet. Maybe if she did it very slowly, she would get it. Then she remembered: "Don't watch your feet!"

Ernie jerked her head up. She was staring right into Ms. Finney's room. Someone was in there. Ernie pressed her face to the window. It was Marcie.

Marcie opened the cabinet under the sink. She took out a bucket. She took out a can of soap powder. She took out a shoebox full of soap bars. She put her shoebag in the cabinet. Then she put the other stuff back. She shut the cabinet door. Then she left the room.

Ernie sighed. Shuffle-hop-cross. Shuffle-hop-cross. She hoped they wouldn't have homework tonight. It was going to take a while to learn "Shuffle off to Buffalo."

CHAPTER 5

The Marcie Move

On Wednesday morning, Marcie wasn't in the crow's nest. When Ernie got to Ms. Finney's room, Marcie was already at her desk. Her shoebag was not under her seat.

Ernie's own tap shoes were in her backpack. Not that she cared much. She had practiced all last night. For what? she wondered. She still wasn't shuffling off to Buffalo. It was more like she was tripping off to Buffalo.

Room 123 was studying "Our Neighbors to the South." This week they were learning about Mexico.

Ms. Finney opened her Mexico box. She pulled out a donkey piñata. She pulled out a shawl with a long black fringe. She pulled out a giant sombrero. She pulled out a poster for a bullfight.

"Olé!" she said. She tacked the poster to the bulletin board. "Who will help me hang the piñata?"

"I will!" said Sammy.

"Me, too," said Jo-Jo.

"Psssst." Tommy poked Ernie's shoulder. "Pass it to Marcie," he whispered. He handed her a candy bar. It was a Mr. Goodbar—Ernie's favorite. There was a note taped to it. The note said,

TO MARCIE

FROM TOMMY

The note did not say, *Now can I try out your tap shoes?* But Ernie knew that was what the note meant.

Ernie tapped Marcie's shoulder. Marcie turned around. The smell of Juicy Fruit gum blew into Ernie's face. Ernie held her breath. She handed the candy bar to Marcie.

Marcie read the note. She leaned around Ernie. She smiled her sweet, sticky smile. She knew what the note meant, too.

"Thank you, Tommy," she said. "But you still can't wear my tap shoes."

Then she turned around. Ernie breathed again.

At practice time, Marcie went to the art closet. She reached behind a stack of paper. She pulled out her shoebag. So that was why Marcie was in her seat so early! She had come early to hide her shoes.

"Today I'm going to teach you a new step," said Marcie. "It's called the Marcie Move." She did a fast combination of slaps and hops and shuffles and some other stuff Ernie had never seen before.

Then Jason stood up. He did the exact same thing.

Ernie looked at William. William looked at Ernie.

"What was that?" William asked.

"Got me," said Ernie.

"You two are terrible!" said Marcie. "Watch me again."

She showed them the step again. Ernie still couldn't tell what she was doing. She was moving too fast.

"Like this," Jason whispered. He showed them the step very slowly. "It's not hard if you do it slowly."

Ernie and William copied him. They both got it! But when Ernie tried to do it fast, she got all tangled up again. So did William.

"Just do it slowly for a while," whispered Jason. "Till you really know it. Then you can speed it up."

Marcie bounced her yellow hair. "You're not the teacher, Jason," she said. "I am. I'm the only one who takes lessons. So there."

"But I know how to do it, Marcie," whispered Jason. "Couldn't I try it just once in your shoes?"

"Quit asking me that!" said Marcie.

"You should let him once, Marcie," said Ernie. "Jason would be as good as you if he had real tap shoes on."

"He would not!" said Marcie. "He doesn't take lessons!" And she danced away.

William rubbed his lucky rabbit. "She makes me mad," he said. "You wouldn't be as good as her if you had tap shoes, Jason. You would be *better*!"

Ernie thought about that. Marcie's feet moved fast, all right. And her taps made sentences. But so did Jason's.

Ernie watched them dancing. Marcie looked tight—like she was thinking about it a lot. Jason looked all loose and happy—like he wasn't thinking about it at all.

William was right. Jason *was* better than Marcie. William could see it. Ernie could see it. Could Marcie see it, too? Maybe that was why she wouldn't let anyone try her tap shoes. Maybe she was afraid someone would be better than she was. Of course, maybe she wasn't afraid of anything—maybe she was just mean.

At recess, Ernie hurried outside. She didn't worry about wrecking the floor today. She was in a big hurry.

"Come with me," she called to William and Jason. She led them around the corner.

"Duck down," she whispered when they got to Ms. Finney's windows.

The three friends ducked down. Then they lifted their heads very slowly. They peeked in through the window. They watched Marcie hide her shoebag under the sombrero.

"What's she doing?" asked Jason.

"Hiding her shoes," said Ernie. "She does it every morning when she gets to school, too."

"Why?" asked Jason.

"I guess she's afraid someone will steal them," said Ernie.

"Someone in Ms. Finney's room?" whispered Jason. "That's silly."

"Serve her right if someone did," said William.

On Thursday, Marcie brought her costume. Ms. Finney let her show it to the whole class.

The costume was red. It had sequins all over it. It had a short, stiff net skirt that stuck almost straight out. There were black net tights to wear under it. It was beautiful.

"I brought costumes for William and Jason, too," said Marcie. "My teacher always has extra boys' costumes."

Marcie pulled two tall black hats out of a bag. Then she pulled out two short black jackets.

"You have to wear your own shirts and pants," she said.

Ernie felt ready to cry. What was *she* going to wear?

"Jason and I will help you make a costume," William whispered later. They were crouching under the window of Ms. Finney's room again. Marcie was hiding her shoes inside the piano bench. This morning they had been behind the fish tank. "We'll help you all day on Saturday."

Jason nodded.

Ernie felt a little better, but not much.

On Friday, Marcie got another present. This one was from Geraldine. It was Mexican jumping beans. Marcie kept the beans, but she still wouldn't let Geraldine try her tap shoes.

In the morning, she hid them on top of Ms. Finney's closet.

In the afternoon, Ernie didn't know where she hid them. She didn't bother to watch at the window. She was sick and tired of the whole thing!

The afternoon dragged on. Health. Spelling. Art. Today they were all drawing something Mexican. Ernie wished she was *in* Mexico. She wished she was a Mexican jumping bean. Then she would tap faster than Marcie. And she wouldn't need any old costume, either.

Ernie stared out the window. What was she going to do about a costume? Ernie didn't know. Even brain food wouldn't help her this time. Bananas were good for some things. But they wouldn't put a red sequin dance costume in her dress-up box.

"Hey, Ernie," whispered William.

Ernie turned around. William had finished his Mexico drawing. It was a picture of a bullfight. The bull was snorting. Smoke was coming out of its nose.

William handed her a piece of paper. Ernie unfolded it. It was another drawing. This one was a picture of a dancer. She had yellow hair. She had a red costume. She had black net tights. And she was falling down.

45

She looked very surprised.

Ernie smiled. William drew the very *best* pictures.

Finally, the bell rang. Room 123 lined up at the door—except for Marcie.

Marcie bounced over to the piano. She lifted the bench cover. Her mouth dropped open. She stared inside. Then she screamed.

"They're *gone!*" she yelled. "My tap shoes! Somebody stole my tap shoes! And I know who did it, too!" She looked straight at Jason.

CHAPTER 6

A Job for Eagle-Eye Ernie

"You have to help me, Ernie!" Jason was sitting on Ernie's bedroom floor. Ernie's dress-up clothes lay in little piles all around him. "Everybody thinks I stole Marcie's tap shoes."

"Ms. Finney doesn't think so," said William.

"And we don't think so," said Ernie.

Jason sniffled. "That's not enough," he

said. "I want you to prove I didn't do it, Ernie. *Please?*"

Ernie patted Jason's back. "Somebody probably just borrowed them for the week-end, Jason," she said. "They'll be back on Monday. You'll see."

"But what if they aren't?" said Jason. "What if they never come back? Everyone will think I stole them." Two tears slid down his cheeks.

"Ernie won't let that happen," said William. "She has an eagle eye. She will find the thief."

Ernie wasn't so sure. It was true, she did have an eagle eye. Even Daddy said so. Whenever he lost his glasses, Ernie found them. Whenever Mommy lost an earring, Ernie found it. Once, she had even solved a lunch bag mystery. Another time, she had proved that there was no bogeyman in the old yellow house.

But this was different. This was a *real*

crime. Tap shoes probably cost a lot of money. Not as much as diamonds, maybe, but still a lot. Ernie wasn't sure she could solve a real crime.

Jason and William were both looking at her. Ernie looked at the floor. First she stood on one foot. Then she stood on the other foot. Then she threw back her shoulders. She put her hands on her hips. She looked them right in the eye.

"I'll do it!" she said.

"Hooray!" William shouted. "Hooray for Eagle-Eye Ernie!"

Jason wiped his nose on his sleeve. "Thanks, Ernie," he whispered.

They spent the rest of Saturday making Ernie's costume.

Jason cut the sleeves off an old black dress. Then he cut off the neck. Then he cut it short.

William glued sequins all over it.

Then Ernie tried it on. She looked in the

mirror. "It sparkles," she said. "But it sort of just hangs."

"You need a belt," said Jason. He tied some scarves together. Then he wrapped them around Ernie's waist. He tied a big bow at the back.

"And flowers for your hair," said William. He took some flowers off a hat and stuck them in Ernie's hair.

"Maybe Ms. Finney will let me wear the Mexican shawl," said Ernie.

Ernie took the dress off. They stapled ribbons all over it. Then they painted lines onto a pair of white tights.

Finally, Ernie tried on her whole costume. She twirled around in front of the mirror. The sequins sparkled. The tights really did look like net tights.

"Wow!" said Jason.

"You look great!" said William.

"There is just one problem," said Jason.

"What?" said Ernie and William together.

"You have to learn the dance," said Jason. He smiled a shy smile. "But I can help you if you want."

"You will need music," said a voice from the hall.

Ernie and Jason and William turned around. Michael and R.T. were standing in the doorway.

"You look neat, Ernie!" said R.T.

"Really Martian," said Michael.

"So do you!" said Ernie and Jason and William.

R.T. was dressed up like a magician. She had on a tall pointed hat and a tablecloth cape.

But Michael was really amazing. He was wearing a green turtleneck and green tights and a green beanie. Six antennae were fastened to his beanie. Painted ping-pong balls bounced at the end of each one.

His drum was tied to his back. Wooden spoons were tied to his arms. Pot covers were tied to the insides of his knees. A comb covered with waxed paper was fastened around his neck. He held his plastic-bottle rattle in one hand. He held a bell in the other.

"Let's go practice!" shouted William. And they all marched out to the driveway so they wouldn't wreck any floors.

CHAPTER 7

Eagle-Eye Ernie Goes to Work

On Monday morning, Marcie's tap shoes were still missing. Ernie was surprised. She had been sure they would show up. She had been sure that someone had just borrowed them for the weekend. She had been wrong.

Marcie pointed at Jason. "Thief!" she yelled. "You better bring my shoes back tomorrow!"

"That's enough, Marcie," said Ms. Finney. Marcie got quiet, but everyone stared at Jason just the same. Was Jason right? Did they all believe Marcie? How could they?

Ernie remembered when the whole class thought she was stealing lunches. She knew just how Jason must feel. *Awful*, that's how.

Ms. Finney told them more about Mexico that morning. Then Carmen showed some pictures of Mexico City. She had lived there when she was a baby. Then Ms. Finney played some music on the record player.

Ernie had a hard time paying attention. She was too worried. How was she going to prove that Jason was innocent?

Ernie opened her tablet. First she would need a list of suspects. She thought about it. Then she wrote:

> Geraldine
> Sammy
> Tommy

All of them had asked Marcie to let them try her tap shoes. Ernie had heard them. Geraldine and Tommy had even given

Marcie presents. Jason had asked, but he hadn't given her anything. So why was Marcie so sure it was Jason? It didn't make sense. Ernie thought Geraldine and Tommy were better suspects.

Something else bothered Ernie, too. Whoever took the tap shoes would have to tap in secret. They couldn't tap at school. Or in the park. Or on the sidewalk. Someone would see them. That left their own houses.

Ernie knew now what she had to do— follow the suspects home.

Practice that day was awful. Marcie did not dance at all. She just bossed everybody around.

Ernie and William and Jason knew the dance pretty well now, but they were not good enough for Marcie.

"Pick up your feet!" she yelled at them. "Stand up straight! You're doing that step wrong, William!"

"Then show me how to do it right," said William.

"I can't!" yelled Marcie. "Jason took my tap shoes!"

Jason stared at the floor. He wiped his nose on his sleeve.

"I did not," he whispered.

"Did too!" yelled Marcie.

Ernie was glad when practice was over. She was even happier when the last bell rang. Now she could get to work and solve this mystery!

Ernie decided to start with Geraldine. Geraldine always walked home with Carmen. Geraldine went everywhere with Carmen. They were easy to follow because there were two of them. It would be hard to lose them both.

Geraldine and Carmen lived next door to each other. Ernie watched them go inside their houses. Then she hid behind a tree across the street and waited.

Pretty soon, they both came out again. They had changed their clothes. Geraldine was carrying an armful of dolls. Carmen was carrying a blackboard. They went into their backyards.

There were bushes along the side of Carmen's house. Ernie crept behind them. She followed them to the backyard. Then she sat down to watch.

The bushes were perfect. They kept Ernie hidden. She could see and hear everything. But Carmen and Geraldine couldn't see her.

Ernie peeked through the bushes. She could hardly believe what she saw. Carmen and Geraldine were playing school! The dolls were lined up on the grass. Carmen stood in front of them. She was writing on the blackboard. She was teaching them addition!

Then Geraldine taught for a little bit. Carmen helped her. Ernie guessed Geraldine was the student teacher.

Carmen and Geraldine's school went on

and on and on. There wasn't even any recess. There sure wasn't any tap dancing. Ernie was glad Carmen wasn't her teacher.

Ernie's legs were going to sleep. Her bottom was wet from the grass. She yawned. This was *bor-ing*! Ernie liked school all right. But once a day was enough!

Finally, Geraldine's mother called her in. It was almost supper time.

Ernie waited until both girls were inside. Then she jumped up and ran all the way home.

When Ernie got home, Mommy was upset. "Where have you been?" she asked. "I was getting worried!"

Ernie plopped down on a kitchen chair. "I am solving a mystery," she said. Then she told Mommy all about Marcie and Jason and the missing tap shoes.

Mommy sat down, too. She patted her lap. "Come here, lamb," she said.

Ernie climbed into Mommy's lap. She was glad she wasn't too big to fit yet. It was such a comfortable place to be. Especially after a day like this.

"I think it's wonderful that you want to help your friend Jason," said Mommy. "But you are the most important person to me. So we are going to make some rules. All right?"

Ernie nodded.

"First, you must stay in the neighborhood. You are not to go any farther than three blocks away from our house."

Ernie thought about that. Carmen and Geraldine lived only two blocks away. She hoped Tommy and Sammy lived close, too.

"Second," said Mommy, "I am going to give you a watch. I want you to promise to be home by four o'clock." She pulled a watch from her pocket. "Now show me where four o'clock is."

Ernie showed her. Then she put the watch on her wrist. It made her feel grown up.

"And third," said Mommy, "did you ever think that maybe nobody stole those shoes?

Maybe they are still somewhere in the room—just not in the piano bench. Now go wash up. We're having spaghetti for supper."

"Is spaghetti brain food?" asked Ernie.

Mommy smiled. "The way I make it, it is," she said.

CHAPTER 8

The Surprise at Twin Trees

At silent reading time on Tuesday, Ernie didn't read. She chewed on her pencil and thought. Could Mommy be right? Could those shoes be right in this room?

Marcie said she hid her shoes in the piano bench on Friday. But Ernie saw her hide them there on Thursday, too. That meant Marcie had run out of hiding places. She was using the same ones over again.

Ernie opened her tablet to a clean page.

She made another list—a list of the places she had seen Marcie hide her tap shoes. She wrote:

> under the sink
> in the art closet
> under the sombrero
> behind the fish tank
> in the piano bench
> on top of Ms. Finney's closet

Maybe Marcie had gotten mixed up. Maybe she had just forgotten which hiding place she had used on Friday. Maybe she had hidden her shoes under the sink. Or in the art closet. Or under the sombrero. Or behind the fish tank. Or on top of Ms. Finney's closet.

That afternoon at practice Marcie's feet didn't tap. Her yellow hair didn't bounce. Ernie thought her shoulders drooped. Jason's shoulders drooped, too. So did William's. What a bunch of droopy dancers!

"Marcie," Ernie asked, "are you *sure* that you put your shoes in the piano bench on Friday?"

Marcie's shoulders snapped back. She put her fists on her hips. She didn't look droopy anymore.

"Of course I am," she said. She pointed at Jason. "He took them, and he knows it!"

Jason's shoulders drooped even more. Ernie wished she hadn't asked.

After practice, she grabbed William and Jason's hands.

"Come on," she told them. "We have work to do."

She led them back to Ms. Finney's room. She opened the door. Then she stopped in her tracks.

Things were all moved around. Ms. Finney's desk wasn't up front anymore. A stage was there instead. Ms. Finney's desk was in the back of the room by the sink. The other desks were moved around, too.

"Mr. Winkler and Ellen's group must

have done this while we were in the gym," said William.

"Oh, well," said Ernie. "We can still do our job."

"What job?" said William.

Ernie told them her new idea.

Jason looked under the sink and in the art closet. There were no shoes there.

William looked under the sombrero and behind the fish tank. There were no shoes there.

Ernie pushed a desk over to Ms. Finney's closet. She climbed on top of it. She looked on top of the closet. There were no shoes there, either.

Jason looked like he might cry.

Ernie patted his back. "Don't worry," she said. "I still have suspects to follow."

That afternoon, Ernie chose Tommy. It turned out he didn't live far from school at all. In fact, he lived right across the street from Twin Trees.

Twin Trees was one of Ernie's favorite places. They were two huge old pines. Their branches scraped the ground. They were easy to climb, but they were sticky with pine juice.

Between the trees was a secret place. It was almost like a cave. Soft pine needles covered the ground. Pine branches made green walls. It was a perfect place to watch Tommy.

Ernie watched Tommy go inside his house. Then she went straight to Twin Trees. She knelt down to crawl under. But suddenly she stopped. Someone was already there. And that someone was crying!

Ernie didn't know what to do. Probably she should go away. But then how could she watch Tommy?

The problem took care of itself.

"What are you doing there?" the person under the trees cried. "Why are you spying on me?"

"I'm not spying on you," said Ernie, and

she crawled the rest of the way under the trees.

The person began to cry again. It was Marcie! Her eyes were puffy. Her face was red. She looked awful.

Serves her right, thought Ernie. But Marcie looked so awful, Ernie couldn't just leave.

"What's wrong?" Ernie asked.

Marcie hiccuped. "You *know* what's wrong!" she wailed. "My tap shoes! If my mom finds out . . ."

Ernie plopped down on the piney ground. "You mean you haven't told your mom?"

Marcie shook her head.

"But why not?" said Ernie. "That's what moms are for."

Marcie just cried harder.

"But it's not your fault," said Ernie. "She won't be mad."

"Yes, she will," said Marcie. "She'll be mad that Jason is the best dancer, too."

Ernie was quiet. She hugged her knees and

thought. *Her* mommy wouldn't be mad if she lost her shoes. *Her* mommy would think Ernie was the best dancer.

"What about your daddy, then?" said Ernie. "He won't care."

"My daddy lives in California," said Marcie.

Ernie peered out through the branches. Tommy was outside again. He was playing ball in his driveway. He bounced a ball around. Every now and then he threw the ball at a basket over the garage door. He didn't get it in the basket very often, but he kept trying. He would probably keep trying all afternoon. He wasn't the shoe thief. Ernie knew it. Neither was Geraldine. And most important, neither was Jason.

"Jason didn't take your shoes, you know," said Ernie.

Marcie sniffled. "Maybe," she said.

Ernie looked at her watch. It was a quarter to four.

"I have to go now," she said.

"Don't tell," said Marcie.

"I won't," Ernie promised.

Ernie kicked a stone all the way home. Marcie's parents sure were different from hers. Ernie felt she *really* had to find those shoes now. Suddenly she wondered if Marcie had swallowed her gum when she hiccuped. She hadn't smelled Juicy Fruit under the trees at all.

CHAPTER 9

With or Without Magic

"Attention, class," Ms. Finney said right after the Pledge of Allegiance on Wednesday, "Marcie has something she would like to say."

Marcie stood up. She walked to the front of the room. Her eyes were puffy. Her hair was messy. She looked even worse than yesterday.

Marcie cleared her throat. She stared at the floor. Her hands made fists at her sides.

"I'm sorry," she said. "Whoever took my tap shoes, *please* bring them back. I will let you try them. I will let everyone try them."

Then she ran back to her seat.

Ernie tapped Marcie on the shoulder. Marcie turned around. Ernie handed her a small brown paper bag.

"Here," she said. "In case I don't find your shoes. You can make some like ours with these."

Marcie held out her hand. Ernie emptied the bag into it. There were six washers and six tacks.

"Thank you, Ernie," Marcie whispered.

That afternoon was Sammy's turn. Ernie followed him out the door. She watched him climb onto an orange school bus. Too bad! She couldn't follow Sammy. If he took the bus, he lived way farther away than three blocks.

Ernie kicked a stone all the way to the

Martian clubhouse. She needed help. Four heads were better than one.

Michael was already there. He was wearing his headphones. He was talking to Mission Control.

"Venus is attacking Path A," he said. "Path B is in a meteor shower. Tell me a new path to Jupiter. Over."

Just then, R.T. and William came in. R.T. was wearing her tablecloth cape. She was carrying Ralph underneath it. William was wearing R.T.'s pointed hat.

"Ask Mission Control where Marcie's tap shoes are," Ernie told Michael.

"That is an Earth problem," said Michael. "Mission Control can't help."

"Maybe it was magic," said R.T. She scratched Ralph behind his ears. "Maybe a real magician made the tap shoes disappear."

'There aren't any real magicians in Ms. Finney's room," said William.

"Hmmmm," said Ernie. "There aren't any real magicians. But the tap shoes could have disappeared without magic—and without a thief, too!"

"Huh?" said Michael.

"How?" said William and R.T.

"Maybe they fell behind Ms. Finney's closet," said Ernie.

"Or behind the fish tank," said William. "Then they would be in back of the book shelves."

"Or off the shelf in the art closet," said Ernie.

R.T. chewed her braid. "Why not just behind the curtains? Or underneath the bean-bag chair?"

Ernie jumped up off her orange crate. "You're right, R.T.! They could be any-where! Behind the encyclopedia. In a plant pot. Maybe Marcie didn't hide her shoes in *any* of the places she used before. Maybe she hid them in a brand-new place. A place so good, even she forgot where it was!"

"So now what?" said William.

"So now we search," said Ernie. She looked at Michael. "*All* of us. Meet me on the playground early tomorrow. We are going to find those shoes!"

"Good," said Michael. "Now we can go to Jupiter. Fasten your seatbelts, everyone."

CHAPTER 10

The Surprise Solution

On Thursday, Ernie raced through break-fast. She grabbed her backpack. She ran out the door.

Ernie skipped all the way to school. On the way, she made up a song. She sang:

"Are they near or are they far?
Nobody here knows where they are.
Are they high or are they low?
Today is the day we're going to know."

William and Michael and R.T. were waiting for her on the playground. Jason was there, too. Ernie had called him last night. They all went straight to Ms. Finney's room.

"Goodness," said Ms. Finney. "You are early birds this morning."

"Early woodpeckers," said William.

Ms. Finney laughed. "What can I do for you, woodpeckers?"

"We want to search the room," said Ernie.

"To find Marcie's tap shoes," said R.T.

"So everyone will know I didn't take them," whispered Jason.

"I already searched it once," said Ms. Finney. "But you might think of some places I missed. Can I help you?"

"Sure," said Michael.

With all those searchers, the search went fast. Behind all the books. In all the cupboards. Under the beanbag chair. In all the plant pots. Everywhere anyone could think of. Ms. Finney even looked inside her desk drawers.

Finally, they gave up.

"I'm sorry, Jason," said Ms. Finney. "Those shoes just are not in this room."

"I didn't take them," whispered Jason. "Honest, Ms. Finney."

"I believe you, Jason," said Ms. Finney.

"So do we!" said R.T. and William and Michael and Ernie.

Jason smiled. "I guess it's all right, then," he said.

"Of course it's all right," said Ernie. "But I still wish I could find those shoes!"

By then the bell had rung. The other kids came in. When they were all in their seats, Ms. Finney had a surprise.

"Today is Thursday," she announced. "Parents' Night is tomorrow night. Just one day away."

She stepped onto the stage where her desk used to be. A red curtain hung behind it now.

"Our stage is ready. Today and tomorrow we will practice on it. One act at a time. Carmen's group first, I think." Ms. Finney sat down at the piano. "I will play the piano while each group sets up on stage."

Ms. Finney played a happy marching song. Her fingers ran up and down the piano keys. The first time, the song sounded good. The second time, it sounded funny.

"Hmmmm," said Ms. Finney. "Some of the high notes are sticking. Ernie, will you please go to the music room. Ask Mr. Clausen to come here. He will know how to fix the piano."

Ernie stood up. She walked to the door. Her hand was on the doorknob. Suddenly, she stopped short.

"Ms. Finney," she said. "We don't need Mr. Clausen."

She walked over to the piano. She lifted the top.

"I can fix this piano," she said.

The whole class stopped talking. They all stared at Ernie.

Ernie grinned straight at Jason. She reached inside the piano. Then she pulled out Marcie's shoebag.

*   *   *

Room 123 erupted.

"Hooray for Ernie!" "Yay, Eagle Eye!" "Hip hip hooray!"

Even Jason was shouting. "I knew you'd find them, Ernie. I knew it! I knew it!"

Marcie was shouting, too. "Who put them there?" she yelled. "I want to know who put them there!" She was back to her old self again.

Ernie laughed. "You put them there yourself, Marcie," she said. "Then you forgot where you put them."

"I did not!" shouted Marcie.

Ernie just smiled. She knew she was right. And she knew Marcie knew it, too.

Marcie's face turned red. She stared at the floor for a minute. Then she shrugged her shoulders and looked up. She grinned back at Ernie.

"I guess I'm a pretty good hider, huh?" she said.

Everybody laughed.

CHAPTER 11

The Big Night

Everyone said it was the best Parents' Night ever.

Stump the Parents really did stump the parents. Ernie's favorite was the trick they played on William's dad. They blindfolded him. They held his nose shut. Then they made him taste an apple and a raw potato and an onion. He couldn't tell which was which!

The Magic Marvels did some really great

magic tricks. Ralph jumped out of R.T.'s hat, all right. Then he jumped right off the stage. But Jo-Jo's trick was perfect. He sat on a chair. He put an egg in his mouth. He pretended to swallow it. (It was really still in his hand.) He clucked like a chicken for a little while. Then he stood up. There was an egg where he had been sitting! It looked exactly as if he had layed it!

Jupiter Jive played fifteen instruments with just four kids. And the Tip-Top Tappers didn't miss a step.

The parents clapped and clapped.

"You were wonderful!" said Mommy.

"My daughter, the dancer!" said Daddy.

Jason's mom hugged him. "What a talent you have!" she said. "I never noticed it before. Would you like to take lessons?"

Jason just nodded. He looked too happy to say anything.

William's dad clapped William on the back. "You were great, son!" he said.

"You missed a step, Marcie," said Marcie's mother.

Ernie's daddy turned around. "I didn't see it," he said. "Marcie, you were super. And to think you taught everyone else!" He reached out his arm. "I'd like to be the first to shake your hand."

Marcie shook hands, beaming.

When it was all over, Ernie and Mommy and Daddy walked home. Ernie held their hands.

"I'm glad I'm yours," she said.

"So are we," said Mommy and Daddy together.

The stars were twinkling in the sky. Ernie felt like she was twinkling, too.

BUY ONE **EAGLE-EYE ERNIE**™ MYSTERY AND RECEIVE ONE FREE!

The adventures continue... but not the cost!

Regulations:

1. All coupons must include proof of EAGLE-EYE ERNIE purchase.
2. Limit one free book per household.
3. Offer expires May 31, 1991
4. Entries must be legible. Not responsible for lost or misdirected mail.
5. Simon & Schuster employees and their families are not eligible.